For Nick and Katrina,
as you embark on a new adventure
— K.D.

For Sam Ledbetter Iscoe
— L.J.

The illustrations for this book were made with pencil and watercolor.

Cataloging-in-Publication Data has been applied for and
may be obtained from the Library of Congress.

ISBN 978-1-4197-4552-2

Text © 2021 Kelly DiPucchio
Illustrations © 2021 Lita Judge
Book design by Heather Kelly

Printed and bound in China
10 9 8 7 6 5 4 3 2

Abrams Books for Young Readers are available at special discounts when purchased in quantity
for premiums and promotions as well as fundraising or educational use. Special editions can also be
created to specification. For details, contact specialsales@abramsbooks.com or the address below.

ABRAMS The Art of Books
195 Broadway, New York, NY 10007
abramsbooks.com

FORTY WINKS

A Bedtime Adventure

words by
Kelly DiPucchio

pictures by
Lita Judge

Abrams Books for Young Readers · New York

"*It's time for bed!*" the Wink parents said.
Their routine was the same every night.
Mama and Papa lined up their big brood,
all thirty-eight children in sight:

Wilma,   Winky,   Walter,   Stinky,   Itty-bitty Boo,

Gabby,   Gary,   Tiny,   Terry,   Stella,   Little Stu,

Murphy, Moxie, Moe,

Larry,   Lucky, Lulu,   Bucky,

Tucker, Tipper, Scooter, Skipper, Freckles, Farley, Flo,

Beamer, Binky, JoJo, Dinky, Hilda, Hide, and Seek,

Skitter, Scatter, Pitter, Patter, babies Pip and Squeak.

The loud, hungry pack was served up a snack
of cider and crumb cakes and cheese.

Some sipped and some slurped,

some gobbled and burped,

while others said "thank you" and "please."

A puddle-long path led
them straight to the bath

and sudsy, warm
water-filled pails.

Pa leaned in the tub
to rub, dub, and scrub

all thirty-eight
noses and tails.

Now clean and well fed, they all dressed for bed
in snug-fuzzy flannels and caps.

Some little ones cried, while the bigger ones tried
to help with the diapers and snaps.

Next, every small Wink scampered off to the sink,
brushing and flossing in pairs.

"You look *squeaky* clean!" Papa beamed at his team
as they gathered in cush-cozy chairs.

They were each read a book (what a long time *that* took!),

then Pitter, he pleaded, *"One more?"*

"Me too!" the rest cried. Mama mumbled, *"Oh my!"*

then she read 'til she snoozed a wee snore.

Now under soft layers, they whispered their prayers,
and each mouse was nuzzled good night.

Some cuddled with blankies

(a few had the crankies),

but each babe was tucked in just right:

Wilma, Winky, Walter,
Stinky, Itty-bitty Boo,

Gabby, Gary, Tiny, Terry,
Stella, Little Stu,
Larry, Lucky, Lulu, Bucky,
Murphy, Moxie, Moe,

Tucker, Tipper, Scooter, Skipper,
Freckles, Farley, Flo,

Beamer, Binky, JoJo, Dinky,
Hilda, Hide, and Seek,

Skitter, Scatter, Pitter, Patter,
babies Pip and Squeak.

All in their places on puff pillowcases,
the fussers were causing a riot.

Some whined and some wiggled,

some kicked and some giggled,

while others said *"Shhh!"* and *"Be quiet!"*

At last, they were sleeping!

Then Moe started squeaking.

"I'm thirsty," the young mouseling said . . .

"Me too!" the rest cheered.
Papa uttered, *"Oh dear!"*
as they all tumbled out
of their beds.

They each took a drink
(what a line at the sink!),

then back to their cradles and cots.

Some bickered.
Some brooded.

Some hiccupped.
Some tooted.

But most settled down
in their spots.

Finally!

Forty Winks closed their eyes
as the sun climbed the skies
and they slept . . .

and they slept . . .

and they slept.

Then . . .

"Wake up!" the kids tugged.

The mouse parents hugged.

"It's time to start over again!"

How many Winks can YOU name?